Artlist Collection
THE DOG

Firefighter Dog

By Howie Dewin

SCHOLASTIC INC.

New York   Toronto   London   Auckland   Sydney

Mexico City   New Delhi   Hong Kong   Buenos Aires

ISBN-13: 978-0-545-07861-0
ISBN-10: 0-545-07861-X

12 11 10 9 8 7 6 5 4 3 2   8 9 10 11 12/0

Designed by Angela Jun
Printed in the U.S.A.
First printing, November 2008

GO TO

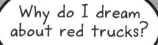

★ Meet Dalton ★

> Why do I dream about red trucks?

He's a shy, one-year-old Dalmatian. He lives out in the country with a nice lady. Dalton has never seen the town nearby. He doesn't know any other dogs. He doesn't even know he's a Dalmatian. But there is one thing Dalton does know. He has dreams—*big* dreams—and they don't make any sense. Why does he dream about red trucks and sirens? Dalton knows it's time to find out. . . .

Chapter 1

There's the big truck!

"Dalton!" I hear someone calling my name. "Get in!"

I jump up high. I am sitting up in the big red truck! Lights are flashing! Sirens are screaming!

We are moving fast! The wind is whipping through my ears!

"Don't be scared!" I shout. "Dalton is coming to the rescue!"

Dalton the Dalmatian woke from his nap.

"Dalton," called Mrs. Marsden.

Dalton shook his head. He felt so confused when he woke up from his dreams. He looked around. He was in his backyard. There was no big red truck. There were no lights or sirens.

"Here is your afternoon treat, sweetie," called Mrs. Marsden.

2

Dalton trotted to the door. He licked Mrs. Marsden's hand.

"You're welcome, sweetie," she said. "Do you want to come inside and watch our stories on TV?"

Dalton looked back at the yard. That was his polite way of saying he wanted to stay outside. He loved Mrs. Marsden, but sitting in the house was boring.

"Okay," she said. "You be a good dog."

Dalton couldn't stop thinking about the truck. Why did he *always* dream about it? He lived on a quiet country road with no traffic. The only truck he ever saw was the white truck that took away the trash. The white trash truck wasn't exciting. The *red* truck was thrilling!

There was only one thing to do. He had to go for a run.

I'd rather be outside.

That would clear his head. Dalton loved to run in the woods. He could run all day long and never get bored.

He looked back at the house. He could hear the television. Mrs. Marsden would never notice if he snuck out through the back fence. Dalton had escaped lots of times. He just had to be home by dinnertime.

Dalton moved quickly. He found the place in the fence where the chain-link had broken

Dalmatian puppies are born without spots.

away from the pole. All he had to do was slip through. The only tricky part was making sure his collar didn't—

"Augh!" Dalton let out a startled gasp.

His collar was stuck on the fence! He tried pulling backwards. He tried pushing through. He yanked his head from side to side. What could he do? He couldn't let Mrs. Marsden find him. Then she would discover the break in the fence. She would repair it. Then Dalton wouldn't be able to take his runs in the woods. He had to figure out how to free his collar without help.

Crunch! Crackle!

Dalton froze. Someone was

coming. He couldn't turn around. The collar
was too stuck. He couldn't even tilt his head to
get a good look.

Crackle . . . snap . . .

The sound was getting closer. Someone was
standing right behind him.

Chapter 2

Dalton couldn't move. He couldn't speak, and it wasn't because he was shy. He was terrified.

"Howdy!" said a shaggy squirrel.

Dalton stared, wide-eyed.

"Relax, Dalton," said the squirrel. "It's me, Sammy."

Dalton's fear faded. He recognized the squirrel. Sammy talked to Dalton all the time. He was very friendly. But Dalton had never been able to talk back to him. He was too shy.

"You're stuck again," said Sammy. "You should really tighten your collar so it stops getting snagged. . . ."

Sammy quickly climbed the fence. He held on to the chain-link with two feet. He used his other two feet to work on Dalton's collar. It took him only a minute.

Dalton was free. He pulled himself through the fence. He looked back at Sammy and tried to speak.

"Free again!" Sammy laughed.

Dalton tried to say thank you. He really did appreciate Sammy's help. But the words wouldn't come. He wished he wasn't so shy. He turned and ran.

Wish I wasn't so shy.

"One of these days, Dalton," Sammy shouted behind him, "one of these days you are going to get up the nerve to say thank you!"

Dalton could hear Sammy laughing as he ran into the woods.

Dalton ran as fast as he could. He lifted his head so he could feel the air on his face. He was already feeling better. It was a beautiful day! He leaped over fallen

Getting to Know You!

In some ways dogs are like people. They need to learn how to get along with others from an early age. It's important that when they are puppies, dogs socialize with other dogs and people. Dogs who don't grow up around others often turn out to be timid (scared) or aggressive (mean).

branches. He splashed in the little creek. He ran and ran. It felt so good!

Dalton didn't worry when he was running. He didn't think about his dreams. He didn't worry about being shy. He would worry about finding his way back home later.

A small pond appeared before him.

I never knew there was a pond back here, thought Dalton.

He stopped running. He stepped into the water and took a long drink. As he lifted his head, he smelled something strange. Something had changed. The air was no longer cool and sweet. Dalton sniffed again. He looked up at the sky. The air even looked different. It had turned dark.

Dalton broke into a run. He didn't know why but he knew he had to find out what was making the sky so dark. He burst through a row of hedges. He was standing in a yard.

A house sat in the middle of the yard. Dark air was billowing out of its top. Yellow and orange flames were coming out of the top windows.

Dalton remembered Mrs. Marsden lighting a match. He remembered the fire in the fireplace at their home. Suddenly, Dalton understood the danger.

The house is on FIRE!

Fire!

Chapter 3

"Fire!" shouted Dalton. He ran toward the house. "Fire!"

He had never seen this house before. He didn't know who lived in it. He had never done anything like this before. But it didn't matter.

He had to help. He had to make sure nobody got hurt.

"Get out of the house!" he barked to whoever might be inside.

I have to help!

Dalton could feel the air as he got closer to the house. He could feel the heat. He jumped onto the front porch. He stood on his hind legs so he could look inside. Through a window, he saw a woman and a little girl.

"Fire!" he shouted. "Get out!"

They couldn't hear him. The woman walked into another room. The little girl was watching television.

With his front paws, he scratched at the window.

"FIRE! FIRE! FIRE!" he howled as loudly as he could.

At last, the little girl turned around. When she saw Dalton, she smiled and rushed to the window.

"Get out! Get out!" Dalton begged.

The little girl laughed. Then she turned around and ran out of the room. Dalton's heart sank. They didn't understand him. He had to do something else. He ran all around the house and barked into every window.

He leaped back onto the porch and howled some more. The front door opened.

"There he is, Mommy!" the little girl said.

"Fire!" Dalton shouted at the woman.

"What's wrong, boy?" the woman asked Dalton.

13

Dalton jumped off the porch. He hoped they would follow him. The woman opened the door slowly.

"Stay here, honey," the woman said.

"No!" cried Dalton. "Don't leave her inside!"

The woman stepped onto the porch. She looked nervous. She moved slowly toward Dalton.

"It's okay, boy. Calm down."

How can she not understand? Dalton thought.

Then, suddenly, the woman looked up. Dalton could see her take a deep breath. At last! She smelled the air. She ran into the yard and looked up at the house. She saw the fire.

"Sarah!" she cried. "Run to me!"

The little girl ran into the yard. Dalton ran to the girl and gently took her sleeve in his mouth. He pulled her back across the yard. He wanted her far away from the fire.

But then the woman ran back into the house!

"No!" shouted Dalton. "NO!"

Dalmatians belong to the Non-Sporting Group of dog breeds.

Before Dalton could follow her, she returned to the yard.

"Fire!" she was shouting into the phone. "At 2764 Pinesboro Road! Hurry!"

The woman ran to her daughter and scooped her up in her arms. The little girl started to cry.

"It's okay," the woman said. "We're okay. You're safe."

Suddenly, Dalton started feeling shy again. Whatever had made him feel so brave was gone. He felt like he had done his job.

Dalton slipped into the woods and hid in some bushes. He watched the fire burn.

"Don't cry. Here come the firefighters," he heard the woman say to the girl.

Sound the Alarm!

Dogs can be heroes in many different ways. They help people who can't see. They help police officers do their jobs. They keep farm animals from danger. But one of the most important things a dog can do is alert people to danger. Because they have such good hearing and their noses work so well, dogs often sense trouble before people do. When dogs warn people about danger, they become heroes. In a dangerous situation, even a few minutes can mean the difference between life and death!

A wailing sound filled the air. Dalton knew that sound. Where was it coming from? Something was flashing. It all seemed so familiar.

Dalton looked out from the bushes. He couldn't believe his eyes. Dalton shook his head to make sure he was awake.

The big red truck from his dreams was coming right toward him!

Chapter 4

The truck screeched to a halt. People in yellow coats and black boots jumped down from the truck. There were so many of them! They moved so fast!

"Lift the ladder!"

"Hose!"

"I'm going inside!"

Dalton watched in amazement.

Who are these people?

The men and women in yellow coats worked together like a machine. They were on ladders in an instant. A big hose came out of the red truck.

"Go!" he heard someone shout.

A huge gush of water shot through the air. It went right into the burning windows. Black smoke puffed out from the house. The fire was disappearing.

Then another truck raced up the road. This one was white and red. The people who jumped from that truck ran to the woman and child.

"We're okay!" he heard the woman say. "Nobody got hurt—"

Nobody got hurt! Dalton heard the words over and over in his head. He knew he had helped. He had made sure that nobody got hurt!

Dalton's heart thumped like he'd been running for an hour. He had never felt so alive! He wanted to run into the yard. He wanted to join the people from the red truck. He knew that was where he belonged!

Before he knew it, the fire was out. The house was damaged but it was still standing. The people in the red truck had kept it from burning down.

"Thanks, thank you so much!" The woman was talking to a teenage boy in a yellow coat.

"You're welcome," the boy said quietly.

An older man approached the woman. "This is Jeremy, ma'am," the older man said, and he pointed to the boy. "He's a junior firefighter, and this was his very first call."

"Wow!" said Sarah, the little girl. "You really are a hero!"

Minutes later, the truck pulled away from the house. Dalton followed the truck. He was careful to stay in the woods. He ran faster than he had ever run before. Finally, the truck slowed down. They had reached the small town. There were houses all around Dalton. It was hard to stay hidden. He ran through backyards and ducked behind parked cars.

The truck stopped in front of a building with huge front doors. The building was as red as the truck. Several people ran out of the building to meet the truck. The people laughed and shouted to one another. Dalton stood still behind some hedges. He watched everything. He saw Jeremy jump down from the truck. Some people shook his hand. Dalton wanted to run to Jeremy. He wanted to meet the hero. But he couldn't get himself to move.

Suddenly, Dalton heard a door slam.

"Hey!" shouted a voice.

Something whizzed by Dalton's head. A shoe landed with a *thud*! Dalton spun around.

A gray-haired man was shaking a stick at him. "Darn stray!" the man shouted. "Get out of my yard!"

Suddenly, Dalton realized he was standing in someone's yard. He had to escape.

He started running again. He moved as fast as he could. He dashed across the street.

"Get that dog!" shouted the man. "I will not let another stray wander around this town.

Digging holes! Eating out of garbage cans!"

At last, Dalton saw a hiding place. He squeezed under an old fence and found himself in an alley.

"Hey, Mr. Farnsworth!" he heard someone say.

Dalton carefully peeked out from under the

FOUND: A LOST PET?

Have you ever found a dog or cat that seemed lost and alone? You may have found someone's missing pet. You can help bring them together by doing a few simple things. Check with your local veterinarians and pet shelters. People sometimes report missing pets to places like that. You could also make flyers and put them up near where the animal was found. Be sure to include a photo of the animal and how to contact you.

fence. Jeremy had come up to the upset man.

"What's wrong, Mr. Farnsworth?" Jeremy asked.

"Another stray! I won't have it. This time I'm calling the county pet-control officer! I'll get this one. You mark my words!"

"I didn't see anything," Jeremy said. "I think it's okay, Mr. Farnsworth."

Jeremy really is a hero! thought Dalton.

He wanted even more to go to the boy. But before he could take a step, someone else spoke.

"Hey, Spot!" came a voice from behind him. "What are you doing here?"

Chapter 5

*R*un! That was the only word in Dalton's head.

He raced to the front of the alley and squeezed under the fence. He stayed low to the ground and hoped Mr. Farnsworth wasn't looking.

There's no safe place! thought Dalton. *I have to go home. But where is home?*

Dalton's ears were ringing. It was hard to tell if mean old Mr. Farnsworth had seen him. When he finally reached the edge of the woods, he stopped to listen. Everything was silent.

He hadn't met Jeremy. He hadn't gotten on the big red truck. And now he had no idea where his house was. He was lost!

Dalton wandered through the woods. He looked for anything that might be familiar. For the first time in his life, Dalton felt tired. He wanted to be home. But he wanted to be at the firehouse, too.

As he walked, he thought about Jeremy. It would be so much fun to be Jeremy's friend and ride in that truck Dalton's heart raced just thinking about it.

I'd like to be Jeremy's friend.

"Hey, Dalton!" called a voice. Then he heard a laugh. "Where have you been?"

Dalton looked up the trunk of a tree near him. There was Sammy the squirrel.

The book *The Hundred and One Dalmatians* has been made into two movies.

"You've been gone longer than usual." Sammy laughed. Dalton stared at him. "Okay, be that way," Sammy said. "But you should get home!"

Dalton looked to the right and then to the left. Which way was home?

"Oh! You're lost, aren't you?" Sammy said. "Well, that's easy. Follow me!"

Dalton was so happy when he finally saw Mrs. Marsden's house. It had never looked so good. He tried to thank Sammy but nothing came out.

"I know! I know!" The squirrel laughed. "You're welcome!"

Before Dalton could try again, Sammy disappeared up a tree. Dalton went straight to his spot under the tree in the yard. He curled up and fell into a deep sleep.

Jeremy . . . the truck . . . the fire and the hose and water . . . the sirens and lights . . .

Dalton's dreams were clearer than ever. Finally he knew what he was dreaming about. When he woke up, he could feel his heart beating in his chest.

"Dalton!" Mrs. Marsden opened the door. "I couldn't find you earlier. Come in, dear."

Dalton's heart sank. He was not in the truck. He was not Jeremy's friend. He lived in a quiet house where nothing ever happened.

He walked slowly toward Mrs. Marsden. He barely lifted his head as he passed her.

"We'll have dinner and then we can watch *Jeopardy!*" Mrs. Marsden said. She patted Dalton on the head.

Dalton couldn't eat. He was too busy thinking about the firehouse. He wanted to go back. He had to figure out how he would get past Mr. Farnsworth and the dogcatcher. He had to be brave.

"You're not hungry, Dalton?" Mrs. Marsden asked sweetly.

Dalton felt bad. She was such a nice lady. But he couldn't be happy here anymore. He would leave in the morning.

"Yeah, Dalton!" Sammy cheered the next morning as Dalton escaped without getting stuck.

Dalton could still pick up his own scent from yesterday. He ran through trees and bushes until the houses started to appear. He was coming into town again.

When he got to Mr. Farnsworth's yard,

he took a chance. He ran across the street and bolted to his hiding place in the alley. He was panting when he turned around to stare at the firehouse. The huge front doors were open. The beautiful truck was parked inside.

Dalton smiled. Nobody had seen him. Now all he had to do was wait for Jeremy to show up. Then he would gather his courage, cross the street, and introduce himself.

But what was that? Some new people were across the street. *No, they aren't new,* Dalton thought. *That's the woman and the little girl from the burning house. What are they doing in the firehouse?*

The woman and child were coming out the front door. Jeremy was right behind them.

"I'm sorry, ma'am," Jeremy said. "But we don't have a Dalmatian. We don't have a fire dog here."

"But he came to our house!" the little girl exclaimed.

"We really must find him," the woman said. "I think he must be a stray!"

"Stray!" cried another voice. Mr. Farnsworth had come out of his house. "The stray is back!" he shouted. "I'm calling the authorities. They'll come to search the area!"

Panic raced through Dalton.

Authorities! What did that mean? he wondered. But he couldn't worry for long.

"Hey, Spot!" The same voice that had

scared him yesterday was suddenly behind him again. "You're back! And it sounds like you're a wanted criminal!" the voice said.

Dalton turned slowly. This time, he wasn't going to run. Whatever was talking to him,

LOST!

It's one thing to find a stray animal. But what would you do if *your* dog or cat got lost? You would do many of the same things if you *found* a stray animal. Let local animal-friendly businesses know your pet is missing. That means contacting pet stores, veterinarians, grooming salons, and animal shelters. You could also make a flyer that tells when and where your animal went missing. Include a photograph of your animal and your contact information. Post your flyers as many places as you can!

he would face it bravely. He took a deep
breath.

The owner of the voice was staring right at
him.

Chapter 6

A strange creature stared at Dalton. It was small and furry. Its eyes were lopsided. Its tail was long and crooked.

"Look," the creature said, "I know I'm a cat and you are a dog, but we can be friends. We can work this out."

The cat's lopsided eyes winked and blinked. She danced around in front of Dalton.

"I don't know what you're doing here, but I'm fine with it. Just don't eat me. That's my only rule. I know you dog-types.

I even know you Dalmatians. You have to get up pretty early in the morning to get ahead of me."

Dalton stared at the crazy kitty.

"Call me Scratch. That's my name. I belong to no one and that's just fine with me. You hear me? Just fine!"

Suddenly, Scratch stopped talking and stared at Dalton. "Why don't you talk?"

"I'm shy," said Dalton.

"Wow," Scratch replied. "I've never met a shy one."

"What do you mean?" Dalton asked.

What a strange cat.

"Dogs aren't usually shy, and Dalmatians *really* aren't shy. Why are you here, by the way? Have you been hired by the firefighters?"

Dalton was confused.

"Hired?" he asked.

"Yeah . . . you know, fire dog, coach dog . . . Dalmatian stuff."

"What does *Dalmatian* mean?" Dalton finally asked. "Everybody keeps saying Dalmatian and I don't know what it means."

"Wow again," Scratch said. "You really don't know who you are, do you?"

Dalton blinked.

Scratch shook his head. "Come with me," the cat said. "I know how to help you."

Scratch led Dalton through a secret exit. They snuck out the back of the alley and stepped directly into the woods.

"It's a bit of a walk," Scratch said. "Just keep up!"

At the edge of a pasture, Scratch finally stopped. Dalton gasped. The most beautiful thing was standing in the pasture. He had never seen anything like it. It was a huge creature. It had short fur except for its tail and neck. It was a mix of different browns. When it held its head up, the hair on its head and neck blew in the wind.

"What is that?" Dalton asked.

"It's a horse," Scratch answered.

"I've never seen anything more beautiful," Dalton whispered.

"That's because you're a Dalmatian."

"What do you know about Dalmatians?"

Dalmatians: The Coach Dog

Before automobiles were invented, horses were the main form of transportation. That meant firefighters traveled in special wagons pulled by horses when they went to fight a fire. Dalmatians were known for their natural affection for horses. They ran ahead of the horses and cleared the way for the rushing fire wagon. Dalmatians also protected the valuable horses from thieves when they were back at the firehouse.

Dalton asked. "You're not a dog."

"Know thy enemy! That's my motto," Scratch said. The cat turned and walked back into the woods. "I make it my business to know about all kinds of dogs. The more I know, the easier it is to stay safe."

"Where are we going now?" asked Dalton.

"Back to the alley, pal. You're not safe out here in the open. Old man Farnsworth wants you taken away to jail! You need to stay hidden."

"What is this place?" Dalton asked as they returned to the alley.

"I call it home." Scratch smiled. "There's a lumberyard on this side."

The cat pointed to the right. "There's a car mechanic on this side. And best of all, there is leftover lunch all over the place!"

"Are you a stray?" Dalton asked.

"You bet! I wouldn't have it any other way," Scratch said. "Freedom!"

"But why don't you have to hide all the time?"

"People don't get so upset about stray cats. I don't know why. Just the way it is. I've always lived in this alley, and no one bothers me."

A door slammed. Dalton jumped.

"Don't worry," Scratch said. "It's just the mechanic."

"Hey!" Mr. Farnsworth's angry voice filled the air. He was standing right on the other side of the door to the alley. He was talking to the mechanic. "I got the dogcatcher here! Have you seen that spotted dog today?"

"What spotted dog?" the mechanic said.

"I'm from Animal Control," said a third voice. "We have reports of a stray black-and-white dog—most likely a Dalmatian. He may have been involved in a recent house fire. Have you seen anything?"

"Yikes!" said Scratch. She spun around to face Dalton. "It's worse than I thought! They don't just think you're a stray—they think you started the fire!"

Dalmatians carried secret messages and emergency-supply kits during World War II.

Chapter 7

Dalton spent the next day scared and hiding in the alley. Scratch brought him food.

"You like peanut butter and jelly?" Scratch asked. She pulled a paper bag under the fence with her mouth.

"I don't know," said Dalton. "I don't think I've ever tried it."

"Good eats!" Scratch exclaimed. Dalton had tried more strange foods in the last day than he had in his whole life.

"Nice to have

company," Scratch said. "The life of a stray can be lonely."

"I've been pretty lonely, too," said Dalton.

"So what are you going to do?" Scratch asked him.

"I mmdon't mmknow," he said, his mouth snapping up and down. "This mmmpeanut mmmbutter stuff is mmmsticky!"

"The drainpipe always has water in it," Scratch said. "That will wash it down."

"I really want to ride that red truck," Dalton finally said after he cleared his mouth. "I think about it all the time. When I fall asleep, I dream about it."

"Well, it makes sense." Scratch smiled. "You are a Dalmatian!"

"But the dogcatcher will get me if I try to introduce myself. Mr. Farnsworth hasn't left his front porch all day."

"He's after you, that's for sure!" Scratch nodded. "And I've seen that Animal Control van two times today!"

Dalton sighed.

"Something else bothering you?" Scratch asked.

"Well, I feel bad about Mrs. Marsden. I'm sure she's worried. I miss her, too. But I have to get on that truck!"

Scratch lay down so she could look under the fence.

"There's Jeremy," Scratch said.

"Jeremy's a hero," Dalton said. He lay next to Scratch so he could look under the fence, too.

"They're all heroes," said Scratch. "Comes with the job. You'd be a hero, too, if you were a fire dog."

The words rang in Dalton's head. *I'd be a hero, too!*

"But even if I could get across the street without being caught, how will I make Jeremy understand?" Dalton asked. "How will he know I'm a hero and not a fire-starter?"

"Not to mention, you're shy," Scratch reminded him.

"Right," said Dalton. "Except with you."

Scratch leaned against Dalton. "Don't

worry. We'll figure it out. You're a Dalmatian. You belong over there."

Dalton and Scratch fell asleep. They had a nice nap together.

The sun was low in the sky when they woke up. The sound of a sniffling cry woke them.

Cats and Dogs: BFFs?

Everyone thinks dogs and cats don't get along. But it's not really true. There are many examples of dogs and cats being friends. And there are things humans can do to make it easier for cats and dogs to get along. It always helps if at least one of the animals is young when they meet. Also, make sure both animals have safe places to go where they can get away from the other. When you introduce the animals, don't leave them alone until you're sure they respect each other.

"Have you seen my dog?"

Dalton recognized the voice.

"He's been gone for two days," the voice sniffled.

Dalton sat up. It was Mrs. Marsden.

He looked at Scratch. Scratch looked at him.

"I haven't seen him," said the mechanic. "But I think some people around here have."

"Really?" Mrs. Marsden sounded excited. Then she let out another whimper. "I don't know what I'll do if he doesn't come home."

Chapter 8

Dalton and Scratch waited for Mrs. Marsden to move on to the next building before they spoke.

"She sounded so sad," Dalton said. He hung his head.

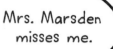

Mrs. Marsden misses me.

"I've never had a human," said Scratch. "But it sounds like she's really broken up about you being gone."

"She is," Dalton agreed.

"So what are you going to do?"

Dalton looked under the fence. He stared at the firehouse. All he wanted was to be a fire dog. He knew that now. But he also knew he had to do the right thing for Mrs. Marsden. She had always been kind to him. He couldn't leave her feeling so sad and alone.

"I can't stand the idea that I'm breaking her heart," Dalton said sadly.

"You're leaving me, aren't you?" Scratch tried to look like she didn't care. "That's okay. Nice to meet you. Don't worry about me. I'm used to making it on my own!"

Dalton nodded. He felt terrible. No matter what he did, someone would be unhappy, and that included him!

It was dark when Dalton finally snuck out the back way that led into the woods. His legs felt heavy. It was so hard to walk away from the firehouse and his dream. He was home before the sun came up.

Dalton curled up under the old tree in the backyard and fell asleep. He hoped he would

Can Dogs Always Find Home?

There are lots of amazing stories about dogs and cats finding their way home from far away. But there are also lots of examples of animals getting lost. So, the truth is probably that dogs are a lot like humans. Some are good at finding their way and some are not. That's why it's always good for a dog to wear a tag!

dream about the firehouse, because that was the only way he would see the big red truck from now on.

The tears Mrs. Marsden cried the next morning were tears of joy.

"Dalton! Oh, my sweet dog!" she exclaimed when she saw him at the back door. "Where have you been? Let me look at you!"

It was good to see Mrs. Marsden. Dalton wagged his tail as he went inside. The food tasted really good. The couch was soft. There was plenty of room. Dalton had to admit it—there were nice things about being home. He forced himself to think only about the good things.

For the next two weeks, Dalton stayed close to Mrs. Marsden. They watched Mrs. Marsden's favorite soap operas. They ate their dinners on little tray tables while *Jeopardy!* was on the television.

"I missed you so much!" Mrs. Marsden would say every day. Then she would smile and give Dalton an extra treat.

Dalton knew how lucky he was. Now he understood that many animals were strays. He knew his friend Scratch had never had it so good. He tried to be grateful for everything he had. He tried to remember how hard it was to be stuck in the alley and hiding from the dogcatcher.

But no matter how hard he tried, he still

missed his days in the alley. He missed being so close to the firehouse. He missed being so close to making his dream come true. He missed Scratch.

During the day, Dalton would spend time in the backyard. Sammy was glad to have him home.

"So there I was, hanging upside down in an oak tree . . . " Sammy never stopped talking. Dalton wondered who the squirrel had talked to while he'd been away.

"I could go for some nuts. Do you like nuts?" The squirrel never waited for an answer because shy Dalton never gave one.

Until one day, Dalton decided he was tired of being so shy. Sammy was hunting for acorns when Dalton finally spoke.

"I was almost a fire dog," Dalton said.

Sammy froze. His squirrel eyes were wide.

"Did you just speak?" Sammy gasped.

"Those days when I wasn't here?" Dalton continued. "I was living in an alley across from the firehouse. I saw the big red trucks. I saw the firefighters. I saw my dream."

"Wow," said Sammy. "So then what happened?"

"One day I saw Mrs. Marsden in town. She was so sad. I knew it was wrong for me to leave her alone."

"No kidding!" Sammy said. "I had no idea! I just figured you went on an extra-long run. I had no idea you had such big dreams."

"Not anymore," Dalton said. The dog lay down and put his head on his paws.

Sammy looked at Dalton for a long time. Then he took a deep breath.

"I know I'm only a squirrel," Sammy said, "but that doesn't mean I don't know a few things. One thing I know for sure—never give up on your dreams!"

"How do you know that?" Dalton asked.

"My great-grandfather lived on a roof in the middle of a big city. He knew it was no kind of life for a squirrel. He dreamed of a better place and he found it. That's why I'm the country squirrel I am today. Because my great-grandfather had a dream, and he didn't stop until he made it come true."

Dalton spent the next few days trying to forget Sammy's advice. It wasn't possible to follow his dreams *and* take care of Mrs. Marsden. Whenever the big red truck came into his head, he ran in circles until he forgot about it. Dalton tried to stop thinking. He just ate and slept and waited for Mrs. Marsden to scratch behind his ears. In the afternoon, he would lie in the sun in the backyard.

That's where he was a few days later when a familiar smell filled the air. Dalton looked up past the trees. The sky was dark. Something was on fire!

Chapter 9

Dalton started running. He didn't have to think about it. It was like something deep inside of him took over. He ran to the fence and slipped through.

"Go, Dalton!" Sammy cried. "Follow your dream!"

Dalton barely heard the squirrel. All he heard was the wind in his ears as he ran. He followed the smell of the smoke. Like the last time, he knew just what he was supposed to do.

As he ran, the air got thicker. The

smell of the smoke was stronger. The sky was darker.

Find the fire! he said to himself. *Warn the people! Rescue the trapped!*

Dalton didn't know how he knew these things, but he did. It was like he had always known.

Instinct Rules!

Many breeds of dogs are considered "working dogs." That means they were bred for certain jobs. The drive to do those jobs is strong in working dogs. It doesn't go away just because a dog isn't being asked to perform the job. Dalmatians have worked as coach dogs and fire dogs for a long time. A Dalmatian's job was not only to protect the horses. They are also known for the work they have done helping firefighters search for and rescue people trapped in fires.

At last, Dalton burst through a line of trees. A house stood before him. He knew from the smell that he was near the fire. Yet the house looked perfectly fine. He ran to the back of the house. He couldn't see anything that looked like fire. But Dalton knew there was a fire somewhere. He had to find it!

He ran around to the front of the house, and that's when he saw the barn. The big red building was close to the edge of the woods, and it was on fire! Flames were coming from a hole in the roof. Dalton could see how close the flames were coming to the woods. He knew there was a danger that the fire could spread.

"FIRE!" he shouted. He ran toward the house.

Please be home! he said to himself. *Someone has to be home!*

He jumped up and put his front paws on a big picture window.

"FIRE! FIRE!" He had never barked so loudly.

He ran from window to window. He didn't see anyone.

"CALL THE FIREFIGHTERS! CALL THE RED TRUCK!" Dalton shouted.

When he got to the back of the house, he saw a cellar door. It was open. Dalton ran down the stairs into the cellar.

"FIRE! FIRE!" he cried.

A man stepped out from behind a door.

"Who are you?" The man looked alarmed. He backed away from Dalton.

"Come with me!" Dalton pleaded. He ran back to the steps. Then he turned to look at the man.

"What is it, boy?" the man said. He had realized that Dalton wouldn't hurt him. He seemed to understand that Dalton was trying to tell him something.

Call the firefighters!

Dalton took three steps back toward the man.

"COME!" Dalton barked. Then he ran back to the steps.

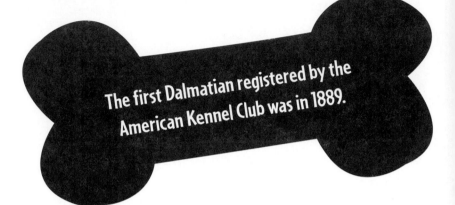

The first Dalmatian registered by the American Kennel Club was in 1889.

"Okay! Okay!" the man said. He followed Dalton. "I'm coming. What are you trying to tell me?"

Dalton ran out into the yard. He turned and waited until he saw the man. Then he ran to the front of the house. Now the man was running, too.

"There!" Dalton shouted. He ran toward the barn. "There!"

He turned back to the man. He wanted to

be sure he was looking toward the barn.

"FIRE!" the man shouted.

Dalton felt a wave of relief.

The man ran into the house. He was calling the firefighters. The red truck would come.

But as Dalton watched the flames leap up from the barn, he wondered if it was too late. His relief disappeared. The flames were nearly touching a branch of a big elm tree that marked the edge of the woods.

Dalton ran back to the house. He and the man had to do something to keep the tree from catching fire.

Dalton started barking some more.

"It's okay, boy," the man said. "I've called the fire department. They will come!"

"The tree!" Dalton barked. Then he saw a long tube just like the firefighters used. It was the thing that shot water at the fire. It was attached to the house. It was smaller than the ones the firefighters used but it looked like the same thing.

"Hose!" Dalton barked. He ran to the hose and grabbed it in his mouth.

We have to spray water until the red truck gets here! thought Dalton. *We can't wait!*

The man looked at the barn. Dalton saw a change in his face. He understood! He ran for the hose and picked it up. Dalton led the way as they raced across the yard. The hose was just long enough. The man held it up, and suddenly water was shooting out of it. The water rose just high enough into the air to wet the leaves of the tree. Dalton could see little puffs of smoke each time the fire tried to lick the leaves. The water was keeping the tree from catching fire.

WHHIIIRRRR! WWHHHIIIRRR!

Dalton heard the sirens before he saw the truck. Suddenly, he felt the urge to run. Just like before, he knew he had done his job. He started to feel shy and uncertain. He was afraid of the firefighters seeing him.

No! he said to himself. *This time I am not going to run. This time I am going to let them know I helped. I did my job. I saved the barn and the woods! I am a fire dog!*

Dalton kept talking to himself. It was the only way

he could keep his legs from running.

I will not run! I will not run! he chanted to himself. *I am a good dog! I am a fire dog!*

The big red truck appeared. It pulled up to the burning barn. Dalton could see the firefighters. He could see the silver trim of the truck. It was flashing red as it reflected the flames of the fire. It was the most exciting thing in the world.

"Hey!" he heard a voice shout. "It's that dog! The one that was at the other fire!"

I am a good dog.

Dalton panicked. They were after him! They thought he started the fire! All the good thoughts disappeared from Dalton's brain. Now the only word racing through his head was *RUN!*

Chapter 10

Dalton fled into the nearest woods. He ran so fast he nearly tripped. He didn't know these woods. He didn't know where to go. He had to get away.

Dalton passed a pond. He climbed a big hill, and as he got to the top, he stopped. Below him was the town. He searched the buildings that lined the streets. Where was the mechanic? Where was the alley?

Where is Scratch? thought Dalton. He let out a soft whimper. *I need to find Scratch.*

Dalton studied the town until he found a big red building.

There's the firehouse! There's the mechanic's building!

He took off like a shot. Suddenly, he tripped on a fallen tree branch. Dalton rolled head over heels. Rocks and trees whizzed by him as he tumbled down the hill.

"Help!" he shouted. "Scratch!"

But there was no one to help him. He was all alone. He felt a pain in his shoulder. He heard something crack. At last, he stopped moving. He lay still at the bottom of the hill. His head was spinning. He couldn't focus his eyes. He closed them.

Dalton didn't know how much time had passed when he opened his eyes again. But he knew he was all right. He slowly got to his feet and tested each leg. They all worked.

The dog took a deep breath and looked around him. It was a minute before he realized where he was. He was only steps away from the secret entrance into the alley.

"Scratch!" he shouted. He rushed to the opening. "Scratch, where are you?"

He leaped into the alley. There stood his friend, with claws out. Her back was hunched. Her fur was standing on end.

"Stay away!" the cat screamed.

"Scratch!" Dalton cried. "It's me, Dalton!"

"Well, why didn't you say so?" the cat cried. "Are you trying to give me a heart attack?"

"I'm sorry," Dalton said.

The cat took a good look at Dalton. She saw the scrapes and bumps on the dog.

"What happened to you?" Scratch asked.

Some Dalmatians have brown spots.

"I had a little accident, but I'm okay. That's not the problem!" Dalton answered.

He told Scratch everything that had happened. When he finished talking, Scratch shook her head.

"I was just watching the firefighters clean up the truck, Dalton. They got back a few minutes ago. They seem really excited about something," Scratch said.

Dalton and Scratch crept to the front gate of the alley. They wanted to get a good look. Scratch was right. Jeremy was standing in front of the truck. He was talking really fast to a group of people. Everyone was nodding and smiling.

Dalton crept out a little farther. He desperately wanted to hear what Jeremy was saying. Before he knew it, he had pulled himself under the gate

completely. He was no longer hidden.

"That's the dog!" shouted a familiar voice.

Dalton's head turned in the direction of the voice.

Mr. Farnsworth was pointing right at him.

"Finally, I'm going to get that stray!" he shouted.

Mr. Farnsworth moved quickly. He headed straight toward Dalton. He had a stick and a net. He was waving the stick in the air.

"Get back!" Scratch cried.

But it was too late. Jeremy and the other firefighters had seen him.

Will he catch me this time?

Dalton was afraid to move. He knew his dream would never come true now. He was caught. He was going to be sent to the pound. He would never be a fire dog. "Stop, Mr. Farnsworth!"

Jeremy shouted.

Dalton's head turned toward Jeremy.

"This dog is a hero!" Jeremy said. "We were just talking about him! He's alerted families to fires two different times. He has saved lives!"

Dalton couldn't believe his ears. Jeremy said he was a hero! But Mr. Farnsworth wasn't listening.

"He's a stray!" Mr. Farnsworth insisted. He kept coming toward Dalton.

"He's no stray," Jeremy answered. He ran to stop Mr. Farnsworth. "He belongs to Mrs. Marsden out on Warren Turnpike."

Mr. Farnsworth stopped in his tracks. "*Edna Marsden?*" the old man asked.

Jeremy smiled. He gently took the stick and net away from Mr. Farnsworth.

"Would you like to come with me, Mr. Farnsworth?" Jeremy asked. "I'm about to go visit her."

"Why . . . yes," stuttered Mr. Farnsworth. "Yes, I would." He went back into the house for a moment.

Dalton didn't understand. He turned and looked at Scratch.

"Why is he nice all of a sudden?" Dalton asked Scratch.

"I think he has a crush!" Scratch giggled. "I think your owner has a boyfriend!"

Just then, Jeremy bent down in front of Dalton. Dalton's heart raced with excitement.

"You are a brave dog. It's an honor to meet you," Jeremy said.

"Nice to meet you, too," Dalton said. But Jeremy only heard a small yip.

"Would you like to be our official fire dog?" asked Jeremy.

This time Dalton

leaped to his feet and barked. He ran in circles and jumped up on Jeremy. He couldn't contain his joy.

"I guess that's a yes!" said an older firefighter standing behind Jeremy.

"I guess it is." Jeremy laughed.

"Yeah, Dalton!" Scratch called out.

Dalton turned back to his friend. "What about you?" he asked.

"I don't think they have fire cats," Scratch said.

Dalton stood behind Scratch. He nudged her forward with his nose. He pushed her right up to Jeremy. He barked again.

"You want us to have a fire cat, too?" Jeremy asked.

"Yes!" Dalton barked.

Jeremy turned around. He looked

> A fire dog? Me?

at the other firefighters. Everyone looked surprised.

"Well, okay!" said the older firefighter. "We could use a mouser."

Dalton had never felt so much happiness. There was only one more thing he had to do.

"Let's go talk to Mrs. Marsden," Jeremy said.

Just then, Mr. Farnsworth returned. His hair was neatly combed. He carried flowers.

Jeremy smiled at the man. "Would you like to tell Mrs. Marsden that you're the one who found her dog, Mr. Farnsworth?" Jeremy asked.

Mr. Farnsworth smiled and said, "I haven't seen Edna in twenty years. . . . "

When they arrived at Mrs. Marsden's house, Mr. Farnsworth rang the doorbell. Dalton couldn't believe it. Mrs. Marsden smiled when he gave her the flowers.

Then Jeremy explained everything that had happened.

"Your dog is a real live hero," Jeremy said.

"My Dalton?" asked Mrs. Marsden. She stared

at her dog. Dalton knew she was proud.

"That's right," said Mr. Farnsworth, "a real hero."

"We would really like Dalton to be the official fire dog if it's okay with you," Jeremy said.

Dalton held his breath. He waited to hear

what Mrs. Marsden would say.

"Could he still visit me on his days off?" Mrs. Marsden asked.

"Of course," said Jeremy.

Dalton barked and licked Mrs. Marsden's hand.

"Edna," Mr. Farnsworth said shyly, "if you'd like, you could visit me. We could sit on my porch together. I'm right next to the firehouse, so you'd see Dalton all the time."

Mrs. Marsden smiled again.

Sirens and flashing lights broke the awkward silence. Dalton looked out to the road. The big red truck had arrived at his house.

"Dalton," said Jeremy, "it's time for your first official fire truck ride!"

Dalton ran to the truck. He couldn't believe it was happening. Jeremy lifted him up to the seat next to the driver. Scratch was already there waiting for him.

"Fire dog!" Scratch shouted. "Look at you!"

Dalton had no words. He sat tall in his

seat. The truck began to pull away from Mrs. Marsden's house. The lights began to flash. Just before the siren began to sound, Dalton heard someone call his name.

He looked up at the tree in Mrs. Marsden's front yard. Sammy was jumping up and down on a high branch.

"Go, Dalton!" the squirrel shouted. "Always follow your dreams!"

Dalton knew that he had.